MY AMERICAN JOURNEY

From Telegraph to Lightbulb

with Thomas Edison

BY DEBORAH HEDSTROM-PAGE

ILLUSTRATIONS BY SERGIO MARTINEZ

FROM TELEGRAPH TO LIGHTBULB

© 2007 by B&H Publishing Group
Illustrations © 1998 by Sergio Martinez

ISBN: 978-0-8054-3271-8

Published by B&H Publishing Group
Nashville, Tennessee

Dewey Decimal Classification: F

Subject Heading: EDISON, THOMAS \ INVENTORS—FICTION

Unless otherwise stated, all Scripture references are from the Holman Christian Standard Bible™
Copyright 1999, 2000, 2002, 2003 by Holman Bible Publishers.

1 2 3 4 5 6 7 8 9 10   11 10 09 08 07

Foreword

Flip a light switch. Plug in a sound system. Press the buttons on a TV remote. These things get done every day, and no one ever gives them a single thought. But long before we were flipping, plugging, and pressing, Thomas Edison was thinking about the things that would make them work.

The way things worked and could work fascinated Mr. Edison. Though a trained telegrapher, he didn't want a regular job. He wanted to invent all day, everyday. So at twenty-three years old he opened his first invention factory. During the next sixty years, he'd file 1,093 patents on inventions. Many of them directly affect us today. The light switch we flip— Edison invented the first long-burning light bulb and built the first power system that put electricity into homes. The sound system we plug in—he designed the first phonograph that recorded music and voices. And the buttons we press on our TV remote—he invented the first moving pictures! In *From Telegraph to Light Bulb with Thomas Edison,* you'll enter Mr. Edison's invention world. Like a fly on the wall, you'll hear the zap of electric wires, wrinkle your nose at the smell of chemical jars, and see bits and pieces transformed into life-changing inventions. As in all *My American Journey* books, a fictional character will lead the way, but in this book he's only half fiction! When Mr. Edison was a teenager, he actually saved a three-year-old child from death. That child was Jimmie Mackenzie. Building on this true fact, I start the fiction eleven years later when Jimmie's parents decide to apprentice their son to the man who saved his life. Leaving home for the first time, Jimmie gets on a train headed for New York City. We join him as the big steam engine screeches to a halt in the middle of a sprawling depot. The conductor yells, "Passengers departing in New York City, please gather all your belongings."

Prologue

New York City, 1874

For the tenth time Jimmie set his two travel bags on the ground but then picked them up again. Should he wait somewhere else? There were so many trains, so many people. Looking around the huge railroad station, he thought, *What should I do?*

The other passengers who had gotten off in New York had all been met by others or had found hackneys to take them to their destinations. But amid the bustling people, no one had come searching for a James Mackenzie from Mount Clemons, Michigan.

Glancing around again, Jimmie spotted a slender, bearded man in a dark suit hurrying through the crowds toward him. He felt a surge of hope as the man stepped up to him and asked in a slight British accent, "Would you be James Mackenzie?"

When Jimmie nodded yes, the man took a deep breath and let it out. "Very good! I am Charles Batchelor. Mr. Edison sent me."

Relief loosened every muscle in Jimmie's body, and he plopped his bags down to reach up and take Mr. Batchelor's hand. Pumping it up and down, he mentally thanked the good Lord that he wouldn't be spending the night on a depot bench!

"I am so sorry to be late," Mr. Batchelor said after getting back his well-shook hand. Taking a white handkerchief out of his coat pocket, he removed his derby and wiped his brow. "We were working on an electric pen, and time slipped away. I hope I did not give you a fright."

Smiling, Jimmie assured the man he was fine as they walked toward a waiting carriage. Lifting his bags into the back and then climbing inside, he wondered for the hundredth time what his

apprenticeship to an inventor would be like. *Maybe I'll invent a talking telegraph or a flying machine!*

His excited thoughts made Jimmie a bit shaky when he remembered Mr. Edison and what his father had said about him. "I met Tom when he was fourteen or so—about your age," his father had told him. "He'd lost his job as a newsboy on the Grand Trunk Railroad after accidentally setting one of the baggage cars on fire. Took to hanging around my telegraph station. A real bright lad, that one. He taught himself Morse code and even built a telegraph line between his house and a friend's. He was always fooling with chemicals and electricity and such too."

Well, at least an electric pen can't catch on fire, Jimmie thought—*or can it?*

"It's ten miles to the factory in Newark, so you only have a spot more traveling to do."

Mr. Batchelor's comment startled Jimmie out of his thoughts. "New Jersey is that close?" he asked.

"Yes," Charles Batchelor said while maneuvering the horses around a freight wagon. "That's the main reason Mr. Edison chose Newark for the factory. The close shipping and rail yards allow us to get the materials we need while the city's population provides plenty of workers and its foundries can make items to our design."

Jimmie hadn't thought much about what was needed to run an invention factory, but listening, he realized it was a lot!

Once past the busiest streets, Mr. Batchelor turned and looked at the factory's new apprentice. "I understand Mr. Edison saved your life," he said.

Jimmie nodded. "I don't remember much, but I've heard my parents tell the story many times."

"What happened?" Batchelor asked.

"I was only three years old, but my father often took me to his telegraph station at the Mount Clemens train depot," Jimmie said. He scooted to the edge of the carriage seat so his companion could hear him more easily. "Well, one day while my father worked, I got onto the railroad tracks. I climbed over one of the iron rails and started to play with the gravel between the wooden ties."

Noticing that he had Mr. Batchelor's full attention, Jimmie made a dramatic pause before continuing. "Just then a two-ton freight car started rolling toward me. The brakeman on the car's roof cranked the brakewheel, but the car just kept moving closer. The man yelled and started waving his hands. I saw him, but I didn't understand the danger. I just held up a pretty rock for him to see.

"At that moment my doom seemed sure," Jimmie explained. "Just a few more feet, and I'd be crushed.

"Suddenly Mr. Edison came out of nowhere and dashed in front of the rolling freight car. He scooped me into his arms then half-jumped and half-tumbled out of the way."

"My goodness!" Mr. Batchelor said. "I had no idea. Was either of you hurt?"

"We got a few gravel cuts and bruises, but nothing else," Jimmie answered. "His saving me that day is why my father offered to teach Mr. Edison telegraphy. Actually he knew a lot already, but he needed speed. To be a telegrapher, you've got to understand the dots and dashes real fast, and you've got to write quick too."

Jimmie would have gone on a bit more, but just then Mr. Batchelor pointed and said, "This is Ward Street. The factory is just down the block."

A large, four-story, brick building with lots of windows stood in the direction of Mr. Batchelor's pointing hand. Jimmie noticed a couple of trees off to one side, but nothing else softened the stern-looking structure. As the horses clip-clopped to a stop in front of it, neither Jimmie nor his companion said anything.

Walking toward the front door, all the excitement Jimmie had felt while telling the story of his rescue suddenly turned into a big knot in the middle of his stomach. In a few minutes he was going to meet Thomas Alva Edison, the man who had saved his life—and the man who would control the next four years of it!

Chapter One
NEWS BUTCHER

Newark, New Jersey

Every step creaked and groaned as Jimmie followed Mr. Batchelor up the three flights of stairs to the fourth-floor research laboratory. Tense and a bit afraid, Jimmie kept looking around. Lots of men and equipment filled each floor—more than he had imagined

As if reading his thoughts, Charles Batchelor said, "Mr. Edison employs fifty men, and we are working on about the same number of projects."

When they reached the third floor, Jimmie forgot his uneasiness. He spotted something that looked like a flying machine. "Golly, does it fly?" he burst out.

Charles shook his head no. "Mr. Edison had some good wing ideas, but so far it has never worked."

Thoughts of flying filled Jimmie's mind until he left the last creaky step behind and entered the fourth floor. Seeing the rows of tables and all the working men, he wondered, *Which one is Mr. Edison? They all look alike—white shirts with high, starched collars, bow ties, and dark aprons.*

Unconsciously, he stood up taller. Big shelves along the walls were filled with bottles of every shape and size. But Jimmie barely noticed them as he followed Mr. Batchelor through the maze of tables. Just ahead was his future!

Approaching a back table, Jimmie saw a man about his height with brown, tussled hair. He was fiddling with something that looked like a pen, but instead of marking the paper beneath it, the gadget was punching little holes into it. He couldn't help noticing that the man's hands were stained yellowish brown. He also had some sort of stains on his pants, and his shoes were scruffy. Jimmie relaxed a little. If this was Mr. Edison, he hardly looked like an exalted inventor. As a matter of fact, he reminded Jimmie a little of his father. *Surely he can't be too bad*, Jimmie thought.

"Al, here's James Mackenzie," Charles Batchelor said loudly, almost yelling. "I was late arriving at the station, but I found the chap right off."

At first Jimmie didn't think the man had heard the introduction because he kept working. But when the pen's needle tip finally went up and down faster, he looked up. A lock of hair fell over one side of his forehead, but he didn't brush it aside. Instead he glanced up and down at Jimmie and said, "You've grown into a tall young man, but I can still see the little tyke I knew in you." Then turning to his friend, he said, "Batch, I've got the ink working. See what you can do to control the flow while I talk with young Mackenzie."

While Mr. Batchelor traded his coat for a dark apron, Jimmie followed his new master to a cubbyhole office stacked with papers. Sitting down in a chair and pointing to one for Jimmie, Thomas Edison said, "So you want to be an inventor?"

"I like taking things apart and figuring out how they work," Jimmie answered.

"You'll need to speak up," Mr. Edison said. "I'm a bit deaf. Folks have to yell for me to catch what they're saying, but I don't mind. Not hearing well helps me concentrate when I'm working."

Jimmie repeated his answer more loudly about taking things apart, and this time his new employer nodded. "Growing up around telegraphs and the like, I'm not surprised," he said. "That's why I told your father I'd take you on. Besides, he did me a great service in my younger days, teaching me telegraphy. Got me where I am today."

Maybe it was the tension, or the long trip, or telling Mr. Batchelor about his childhood rescue—but whatever the cause, Jimmie blurted out a question he never would have asked if he weren't so tired and nervous: "Is it true you caught a baggage car on fire?"

Mr. Edison laughed and leaned back in his chair. "I'm afraid so. I was only twelve when it happened, but I'd already been doing lots of experiments," he began. "I had landed a job as a news butcher on the Grand Truck about the time Abraham Lincoln got elected president. I'd go through the cars calling to the passengers, 'Peanuts, apples, sandwiches . . . read the *Detroit Free Press!*' "

As Mr. Edison told his story, he called out his wares in much the same way as he must have done as a boy. Jimmie pictured a younger version of the man in front of him going from rail car to rail car, selling stuff.

"Traveling the line left me with lots of time on my hands," Mr. Edison continued. "I'd been selling newspapers—the *Detroit Free Press*—and was able to get hold of some castoff type, composing sticks, ink, and paper. In the baggage car, I set up a flatbed press and soon was selling my own newspaper, which I called the *Grand Trunk Herald*—sold it for three cents a copy."

"Did your press catch fire?" Jimmie asked, his tension and fear forgotten.

"No, that wasn't it," Mr. Edison answered. "But I had set up my printing press in a baggage car. And a bit later, when I asked to set up a laboratory there, the conductor agreed since my printing press hadn't been a problem."

Having just seen a baggage car, Jimmie easily imagined Mr. Edison setting up a makeshift laboratory in one, moving in a table and loading it with jars and wires and such.

"Things went along fine until one day the train lurched," Mr. Edison said. "The jolt sent my chemicals tumbling. They mixed together and burst into flames. I helped put out the blaze, but not before it ruined the inside of the baggage car."

Jimmie leaned forward in his chair. "What did they do to you?" he asked.

"Threw me off the train," he answered. "I had to get another job selling papers at the railway stations. That's when I met your father and pulled you off the tracks."

Jimmie wanted to ask more questions, but just then Mr. Edison stood up. "I'm going to have someone take you to my home. My wife, Mary, will help you get settled and give you some supper. I'm spending the night at the lab; tomorrow I'll expect you here around noon."

Another man named Joseph Murray took Jimmie to Mr. Edison's home. Later, after a good dinner and a warm bath, Jimmie climbed into bed. At first he couldn't get to sleep, excited at the thought that tomorrow he'd start learning to be an inventor. But the long trip and tense day finally closed Jimmie's eyes. That night he dreamed of flying machines and hole-poking pens.

Chapter Two
99 PERCENT PERSPIRATION

Newark, New Jersey, 1875

Jimmie hooked up another piece of wire to the double telegraph switches. Simultaneously he tapped out a short message on both levers. A few seconds later, Joseph called to him from the opposite end of the table, "One message still comes in weaker than the other."

Exasperated, Jimmie pulled the wires from the double switch and said, "This will never get better! It's useless! You can't send two clear telegraph messages and receive both of them at the same time."

"Nothing is useless, James."

Hearing the now-familiar voice of his boss, Jimmie turned on his stool and said, "But Mr. Edison, this is the twenty-third relay we've tried. Nothing improves the signals."

"Only twenty-three?" he answered. "Don't be discouraged. Every wrong attempt discarded is another step forward. You haven't failed twenty-three times. You've just eliminated twenty-three possibilities."

Jimmie nodded wearily. He'd heard this lecture about failures being steps forward at least a dozen times since starting work at the factory nine months earlier.

"You've been at this for hours," Mr. Edison said. "Go get a drink of water and grab a bite of cheese."

Jimmie got off his stool and trudged his way back to the water bucket.

Picking up the dipper, he plunged it into the clear liquid. Instantly, a jolt shot up his arm. Dropping the dipper, he let out a squeal.

Just then everybody broke out laughing. Bewildered and a little mad, Jimmie called out, "What's the big idea? What's going on?"

Francis Jehl stopped laughing long enough to say, "I think Mr. Edison thought you could use a charge of energy."

Turning back to the water bucket, Jimmie inspected it more closely and saw wires connected to it and the dipper. He quickly realized he'd been set up for one of the boss's practical jokes. He wanted to stay mad but just couldn't. He'd laughed when the jokes had been on others. Besides, he wasn't discouraged anymore. "Well, I guess I did need one," he said with a grin.

Mr. Edison came up and patted Jimmie's shoulder. "That's a good sport. Now remember: Genius is 1 percent inspiration and 99 percent perspiration!"

A short while later, Francis came back to where Jimmie was eating some cheese and bread. "For a minute back there, I wasn't so sure you appreciated the boss's joke."

"For a minute, I didn't!" Jimmie answered. "But it's hard to stay mad at him."

Francis nodded. "It's been that way ever since Mr. Edison was a tramp telegrapher. He was forever pulling pranks on his fellow workers. Heaven knows they needed it with their lousy working conditions and all."

Jimmie wrinkled his face into a question. "What do you mean? My father's place wasn't bad."

"Yeah, but your pop wasn't a tramp telegrapher," Francis said. "He had a steady job for a big railroad. Men like Edison often worked in windowless holes that were infested with cockroaches and other vermin, not to mention rats! That's why more telegraphers die of consumption than anything else."

"That's awful!" Jimmie said. "How long did Mr. Edison do it?"

Francis took a minute to think back. "For about six years," he finally answered.

Jimmie took another bite of cheese and asked, with his mouth full, "Is that where Mr. Edison thought of wiring the water bucket?"

"Yep. Did it on many unsuspecting coworkers," Francis said with a smile while breaking off a chunk of bread and spreading it with lots of butter. "Also jolted a few rats and cockroaches out of this world. He did it by rigging up a couple of wired metal plates. When the creatures stepped onto them to eat a morsel of food planted there by Al, their bodies would complete the electrical circuit, and zap! They'd be fried. He called the wired plates a 'rat paralyzer.'"

"Definitely a fitting name," Jimmie responded as he reached up and rubbed the last tingles out of his own shocked arm.

Two days later Jimmie was still working with Joseph on improving the quadruplex telegraph relay. They now knew forty ways not to do it! "I think we need a library break," Joseph said after their last relay refused to send and receive two strong messages.

"Perhaps reading a few science books will give us some fresh ideas."

"But we can't leave work," Jimmie protested.

"Don't worry. The boss will think it's a great idea. He's been in more libraries than homes!"

In the carriage Jimmie asked about Mr. Edison and libraries. Joseph answered, "As you know, Al is forever reading the *North American Review* and other scientific journals. Well, he's been doing it for years. Even as a tramp telegrapher, he got a library card in every town he worked. He also spent most of his money on used science books. Once went without a coat and even almost got shot because of it."

"Shot?" Jimmie asked in disbelief. "How could he get shot reading books?"

"Actually he was carrying some books he had purchased back to his rented room at three o'clock in the morning," Joseph said as he snapped the reigns to move the horses past another carriage. "He'd gotten off work right after a nearby shop was robbed. So when a policeman spotted Al carrying a bundle that late at night, he hollered for him to stop. But being deaf like he is, Al didn't hear the shout and didn't stop. That's when the policeman fired a shot. Al heard that!"

It didn't surprise Jimmie that his boss hadn't heard the policeman shout. It had taken him awhile to get used to Mr. Edison's deafness, and he was constantly having to repeat stuff. Charles Batchelor told him the boss had lost his hearing while selling newspapers at the train stops. "He was late and running after a moving train but missed the step. A quick conductor caught him by his ear and pulled him up. Al told me he felt something pop inside his head. He said, 'The man saved my life, but I never heard well again.'"

"Mr. Edison sure had adventures!" Jimmie remarked to Joseph. "Obviously, the policeman figured out that he wasn't the robber. But what a scare!"

In the library Jimmie and Joseph got some ideas to improve their relay, and they headed back to Newark, eager to try them. But it wasn't a relay success that made Jimmie dash up the stairs two at a time a week later. It was a letter. Waving the envelope, he hollered, "Mr. Edison! Mr. Edison! I think it's here!"

Hurrying toward his boss, Jimmie gave him the mail with the Menlo Park return address. As the older man opened and read the letter, a smile spread across his face. Then he looked up and said, "Men, we're moving! We've got a new and bigger place for our factory."

Chapter Three
"IT SPEAKS!"

Menlo Park, New Jersey, 1876

Jimmie, I want you and Francis to go to Philadelphia."

Mr. Edison's words startled Jimmie. He looked up from the sewing machine motor he was working on. "What?" he said while his mind flashed with thoughts like, *We've only been in Menlo Park for a few months. All the boxes aren't even unpacked. What about this motor?*

The boss stood in sunlight that slanted through the new factory's many windows and lit up the chemical jars recently placed in the shelves along the opposite wall. "I said I want you to go to the Centennial Exhibition in Philadelphia," Mr. Edison repeated. His hair had fallen across his forehead, but as usual he did nothing about it. "You'll put on display the automated telegraph system, the electric pen, and the autographic press. The exhibition's awards and newspaper coverage will help them sell."

For the next few hours, Jimmie and Francis packed the inventions going to Philadelphia into wooden crates. While working, Jimmie kept thinking about the sewing machine motor's problems. Wrestling with those thoughts in his head and the crates in his hands, Jimmie couldn't help stopping when he noticed the lab's pet raccoon scooping up mercury. The silvery liquid slithered out of the animal's paws scoop after scoop, but the ring-tailed pet kept trying to capture it. "How does he keep it up, Francis?" Jimmie asked. "He scoops for hours on end and gets nowhere. He reminds me of me."

Francis laughed. "Patience, James. You always want every problem fixed yesterday. Solutions will come if you keep at it. Didn't we just install a quadruplex that sends and receives two clear messages a couple of months ago?"

"You're right," Jimmie said as he reached over and scratched the pet raccoon behind the ears. Grinning, he added, "Maybe going to the exhibition

will recharge my patience and energy with less of a shock than Mr. Edison's water dipper!"

But five days later, Jimmie felt more drained than charged. A heat wave had turned America's one-hundredth birthday exhibition into a sweaty, clothes-sticking celebration. That afternoon, after the judges had tried Edison's electric pen and gave it their its scientific endorsement, Jimmie told Francis, "I'd give anything to take off this starched collar and tie."

"I know what you mean," Francis responded as he slid a finger inside the neck of his shirt. "But we must wait until the judges leave, especially since they have the emperor of Brazil with them."

Jimmie watched as the hot, weary judges headed across the exhibit hall. He was just about ready to reach up and undo his tie when suddenly the emperor stopped and spoke to a dark-haired young man. "Professor Bell, I am delighted to see you again. How are the deaf-mutes in Boston?"

Alexander Graham Bell? Jimmie wondered.

After talking a few moments, the judges followed the emperor and dark-haired man back to a display that hadn't been inspected yet. Jimmie told Francis he wanted to see what was going on and trailed behind them.

As soon as Jimmie saw the display, he knew he was right. This was Alexander Bell, the teacher of the deaf who had beaten the Edison factory at inventing a talking telegraph. Even now, Mr. Edison talked of ways to improve Bell's telephone.

One by one, the emperor and judges listened to a receiver while Professor Bell shouted into a transmitter some distance away. "My gosh, it speaks!" one man exclaimed. Another said, "It's the most wonderful thing I've seen in America."

Later, when Jimmie got back to Menlo Park, he told Mr. Edison what he'd seen. "We got awards for all three of your inventions, but many said the telephone was the best thing at the celebration."

"And well it is," Mr. Edison said. "Pity we didn't invent it first. But we'll improve it. From what you've told me, a person must yell in order to be heard. When you finish work on the sewing machine motor, come see my drawings for a better transmitter."

Jimmie stayed busy the next week trying to get electromagnets to vibrate tuning forks. His boss believed the motion of the forks could power a sewing machine. Caught up in his work, it took awhile for Jimmie to notice the commotion growing around him.

"I just put new chemicals in this battery, but it still doesn't work."

"I mixed two chemicals and couldn't even get them to burst into flames."

"My experiments are going haywire."

The comments gradually filtered into Jimmie's motor world. "What's going on?" he asked Batch.

"The boss is checking it out, but it looks as if sunlight has damaged our stock of chemical."

Jimmie remembered how the light shining in the windows had lit up the chemical jars. "What's Mr. Edison going to do?"

"Undoubtedly we'll be turning our shelves into cupboards by adding doors. I also heard Al tell a couple of the men to start doing sunlight experiments. He mentioned writing up the results in the *American Chemist.*"

Back at his table, Jimmie found it hard to resettle into his work. Mr. Edison was always coming up with ideas. Every bit of information, even sunlight on chemicals, had to be used. *What will he think of next?* Jimmie wondered.

Chapter Four
A STARTLING LAMB

Menlo Park, 1877

Jimmie couldn't believe what he was seeing. Mr. Edison was clenching a piece of metal in his teeth! It had wires attached to it that were connected to a telephone transmitter.

"What's he doing?" Jimmie asked Charles Batchelor in a voice not loud enough for the boss to hear. "Trying to shock himself?"

"No, he's listening," Batch answered.

Jimmie took another look at his boss. His brow got a dozen wrinkles in it, and he asked, "With his teeth?"

"It's the only way he can," Batch said. "Being part deaf, he can't hear if a material picks up any sounds."

Suddenly Jimmie's face brightened, and he blurted out, "Oh, I get it! He's feeling for vibrations! If a material does pick up sounds, it quivers with each word."

Batch nodded. "That's right, and I'm glad it works. We can sure use his help."

Jimmie couldn't argue with that. For more days and nights than he cared to remember, they'd been trying to improve Mr. Bell's telephone. The boss had said, "There must be a better way than yelling into the phone. We need to find a material that is more sensitive to sound."

Sometime later Jimmie pushed aside yet another material that didn't pick up sound. He stood up. He felt totally frustrated but only said, "I can't think anymore. I'm off to get some of that ham Mrs. Edison brought over."

Mr. Edison straightened on his stool. "You're going for some of Mary's ham? Would you bring me some?" When Jimmie nodded yes, the boss noticed his apprentice's frustration because he added, "Many of life's failures are people who did not realize how close they were to success when they gave up."

As Jimmie walked back to where the food was kept, he knew his boss was right. The next material he tried could be the one that improved the telephone.

If only I could be more like Mr. Edison. To him, the testing process never gets boring or discouraging! Jimmie thought as he munched on a ham sandwich.

"How is the telephone transmitter coming? You still yelling into it?"

Jimmie jumped at Francis's questions. Off in his own thoughts, he hadn't heard his friend come up. "Yeah, we're still yelling," he said, recovering from his start. "We've tested more than a thousand materials without much success. But the next one could be the right one."

"Hey, you sound just like the boss," Francis said with a short laugh as he picked up a knife to slice off some ham. Pausing in midair, he said, "I just cleaned soot off an oil lamp and was wondering if it could be used for something. Maybe it'll transmit sound!"

Jimmie shared the soot idea with Batch and Mr. Edison when he went back to work. The boss reached up and scratched the back of his head. "Hmmm. Soot contains carbon. Yes, it's possible."

A few days later they were testing the black powder in all kinds of shapes, forms, and combinations. It ended up taking 188 days and 55 nights to finally find the best material. Francis's suggestion had done it. Two carbon disks vibrating against each other carried the sound of a person's voice without his having to yell into the telephone.

Working with sound vibrations must have gotten Mr. Edison to thinking, because Jimmie noticed he kept fooling around with the transmitters. He even sang into them!

During one of his musical sessions, Jimmie heard the boss abruptly stop singing and say, "Ouch!"

"What happened?" he asked.

"The sound of my voice made a wire move and it pricked my finger."

Jimmie was going to ask if he needed something for the wound, but suddenly the boss grabbed a pad of paper and started drawing. A short while later Mr. Edison called to Batch, James Adams, and Jimmie. When they had gathered around, he handed them a drawing of a needle resting on the surface of a cylinder and told them, "This is a phonograph. It should record voices."

The laboratory buzzed with talk of the boss's new idea. As the excitement grew, one of the men, Edward Johnson, said he was going to write the publication *Scientific American* about it.

The next month Jimmie saw it in print. The journal's headlines read, "A Wonderful Invention— Speech Capable of Indefinite Repetition from Automatic Records."

When he showed it to Mr. Edison, the boss frowned. "Get Batch and James. We've got to begin work immediately. Our idea is in print, but we have no patent. Anyone could develop it now."

For twelve days everyone worked on turning the boss's drawing into a real machine. Jimmie made some needles, trying to find one that wouldn't rip foil when pressed against it. Batch put together a crank and sound funnel while James completed a foil cylinder. Mr. Edison constantly helped and checked on each part, nodding or correcting as the machine took shape.

When it came time to test the new phonograph, the boss gathered everyone around. As he called and waved the crew over to the test table, Jimmie couldn't help noticing his bright eyes and high energy. *I've never seen the boss so excited,* he thought.

"Turn the handle, Jimmie," Mr. Edison said. "Keep it at the same speed while I yell into the funnel."

Using the steady ticktock of the laboratory clock like a metronome, Jimmie started turning the cylinder as evenly as he could. The boss bent over the funnel and shouted into it. "Mary had a little lamb. Its fleece was white as snow." At every word of Mrs. Sarah Hale's famous poem, vibrations caused the needle to make a dented line in the thin sheet of foil. "And everywhere that Mary went, the lamb was sure to go."

By the end of the poem, the boss was smiling at the grooves in the cylinder, and he added, "Ha, ha, ha."

The laugh broke up some of the tension everyone was feeling, but Jimmie knew the real test was yet to come. He watched as Mr. Edison lifted the needle and put it back on the first groove. "Turn the crank just like you did before, Jimmie."

Grabbing the handle, Jimmie didn't know why he was so excited. Nothing ever worked the first time. Still he held his breath as he once again used the clock to set his pace forturning the cylinder.

A tinny but distinct voice erupted from the sound funnel, "Mary had a little lamb."

At first no one said anything as the poem continued. Even the boss stood stunned. Suddenly John Kruesi, a German designer, exclaimed, *"Mein Gott in Himmel!"*

"My God in heaven" said it all. The phonograph worked on the very first try!

For the next few minutes everyone was shaking hands, slapping one another on the back, and commenting about the sound quality of the words.

But Jimmie didn't join in when he let go of the handle. He felt dazed. His mind kept repeating, *It worked on the first test. It really worked!*

Chapter Five
THE WIZARD OF MENLO PARK

Menlo Park, 1878

Jimmie had never seen so many people jammed into the laboratory. Most of them had a pencil and a pad of paper. Ever since Mr. Edison had taken out a patent on the phonograph, crowds of reporters had shown up at the lab from time to time to hear demonstrations. On this day Mr. Edison had Jules Levy play a musical instrument called a cornet.

As Mr. Levy performed "Yankee Doodle," Mr. Edison turned the phonograph handle. The crowd whistled and sang along, trying to make a sound that the machine could not record. But when the boss played back the recording, every sound came from the small wooden box.

"It's incredible," one reporter said.

"It's hard to even believe," another commented.

Suddenly the cornet notes, song words, and whistles started coming out of the machine at incredible speed. "My word! How is that possible?" a man said. "No one can play or talk that fast."

"No," Mr. Edison said, "but I can turn the phonograph handle that fast."

The reporters ooh-ed and aah-ed at the phonograph's speed variations until they left. The next day Jimmie read one of the articles written about the demonstration. "The phonograph was equal to any attempts to take unfair advantage of it. It repeated its songs, and whistles, and speeches, with the cornet music heard so clearly over all that its victory was unanimously conceded. Amid hilarious crowing from the triumphant cylinder, the real cornet was shut up in its case."

Happiness over the phonograph's success didn't make Jimmie any less cautious. One morning a few weeks later he checked his table from end to end and top to bottom. He looked for signs of one of Mr. Edison's pranks: wires connected to batteries and jars precariously balanced so they would tip over. He checked his tools and then slowly opened each of his drawers. He couldn't be too careful today. Any joke or prank in the lab was fair game on April first! Last year Francis had put dye on the handles of his tools that turned Jimmie's hands green!

"Hey, everyone, look at this!"

Edward Johnson's shouted words made Jimmie forget about green hands, and he joined the others as they gathered around Ed. He was holding a copy of *The Daily Graphic* above his head so that everyone could see the headlines. Jimmie read, "Edison Invents 'Food Creator.'"

We did? Jimmie thought in surprise.

"Let me see that paper," Mr. Edison said as he walked up to the group. He read aloud about an incredible machine that made food. "Rubbish," he said after finishing the article. "We've invented no such thing. It's ridiculous." Giving the paper back to Edward, he added, "Call *The Daily Graphic* and set them straight!"

Just then Batch, who was usually quiet, spoke up. "Al, I think they know we did not and could not invent such a thing. It's a hoax, an April Fool's joke," he said.

Mr. Edison turned and stared at his close friend and fellow inventor. Suddenly he slapped his leg and said, "You're absolutely right! Quite clever. We must plan a return hoax for *The Daily Graphic* next year."

The rest of the day didn't catch Jimmie on the worse end of any pranks, but two newly hired lab guys dashed outside when they heard a voice yell, "Help! Police! Police!"

Jimmie ran over to the window and looked out. Between laughs, he told Batch, "The boss got them good! He's out there holding what called for help— a phonograph!"

After the pranks and the reporters' visits were over, the lab got busy. Besides working on improving the phonograph, the staff was making a waterproof varnish, a hearing-aid device, and equipment that would prevent static on telephone lines.

Jimmie was used to juggling projects, but the real difficulty was juggling people. Everyone was coming and going. Batch went to Connecticut to do experiments at a clock company. Edward Johnson had gone on tour, promoting the phonograph and the carbon telephone. Another man was testing phone lines between New York and Philadelphia while James Adam went to London to test phones on the British Post Office lines. Even the boss got tied up when a writer from the *Chicago Tribune* came to the lab and interviewed him.

Amid the work shuffle, Jimmie didn't get a chance to see the *Tribune*'s article, but a few days later *The Daily Graphic* caught his attention. On the front page was a drawing of Edison dressed in a flowing robe decorated with pictures of his inventions. A tall, pointed hat and bright light completed the picture of "The Wizard of Menlo Park."

"Hey, boss," Jimmie yelled, "take a look at this!"

When Mr. Edison looked at the paper, he smiled and shook his head. "Sensational but untrue," he said. "All you need to be an inventor is a good imagination and a pile of junk." Then turning, he pointed out a window at the spring greenery popping up everywhere. "Besides, until man duplicates a blade of grass, nature can laugh at his so-called scientific knowledge."

Jimmie knew the boss was right, but he still liked *The Graphic*'s new name for Mr. Edison. As it turned out, so did a bunch of other people. From then on, Jimmie read it over and over:

Wizard of Menlo Park Demonstrates
Phonograph to President Hayes and Congress
Honorary Degree from Union College
Given to Menlo Park Wizard
Grand Prize at Paris Exposition Goes
to Local Wizard

In spite of all the praise, Mr. Edison kept working in his lab, especially on improving the phonograph and making variations of it. One day he told Jimmie, "It's my favorite baby. Once it grows up and becomes a big fella, it will support me in my old age. Of all my inventions, I like the phonograph best."

Jimmie knew it was true. The boss was forever recording Bible passages, popular songs, poems, and shouted exclamations. And in the lab, they were working on a toy phonograph, a hand-held version, a clock-driven one, a phonograph that played a disk instead of a cylinder, and even a phonograph connected to a telephone!

Though the boss obviously loved his new invention, Jimmie knew it would only be a matter of time before he'd tackle something new. He got a clue to what it might be when he overheard Mr. Edison talking with Batch.

"The electric arc lighting we have today is only good for streets or huge buildings. It's too bright for homes," he told Batch. "The gas lighting like I installed here is better, but you still must deal with the danger of flame and fumes. There has to be a way to improve electric lighting."

As the men continued talking, Jimmie went back to work on the toy phonograph he was working on. *Can the Wizard of Menlo Park make better lights?* he wondered.

Chapter Six
THE INSOMNIA SQUAD

Menlo Park, 1879

Clunk-clank, clunk-clank, clunk-clank. . . . The loud, jarring racket jolted Francis awake, and he fell off the bench he was sleeping on. Mr. Edison, Jimmie, James, and Batch burst out laughing.

A variety of emotions flitted across Francis's face—confusion, embarrassment, anger, and finally humor. Like almost everyone else working nights on the boss's latest project, Francis had fallen victim to the "corpse retriever."

The retriever was actually an old soapbox without a cover. Inside was a ratchet-wheel with a slab of wood resting in its teeth. Turning a crank on the wheel hammered the metal teeth into the wood chunk. The noise echoed in the old box and made a horrible racket. Batch said it sounded like "a hurricane in a china shop."

Lately everyone—even the boss—had been dozing off now and then. Sometimes Jimmie would see him curled up on a table with a pile of books for a pillow. No, it wasn't sleeping that caused the others to bring out the retriever or the "resurrector of the dead." It was snoring. Even Jimmie had snored one early morning after working twenty hours straight. But he didn't wake up to a grinding racket; he woke up to a burning bottom! Unlike the retriever, the "resurrector" consisted of putting a combustion fluid under the snorer's behind. When Jimmie woke up, he'd felt intense heat. Jumping off the bench he'd been sleeping on, he'd dashed over to the water tank—and sat in it.

Jimmie didn't get hurt, and neither did the rest of the lab staff. The pranks were a fun way to break the tension of so much work. The long days and nights had begun after the boss had gotten back from a month-long vacation out West. He'd fished and visited Yellowstone Park and come home itching to work on electric lighting.

Other inventors had already developed generators that produced electricity and distribution systems to send it places. Mr. Edison wanted to buy some of this equipment, so he got some investors together and started the Edison Electric Light Company. He bought a new steam engine and two electric generators. Immediately he'd put Jimmie and Batch to work on improving their output of electricity while he invented a meter to measure it.

Using the new and improved devices, the boss put up a lighting display in Menlo Park. He included arc lighting, gas lighting, and a new heated-filament light. For days he had Jimmie take electric and gas readings in order to figure out how much each cost to run.

Everyone at the lab agreed that the new filament light worked best, but Jimmie's figures also showed it cost way more than the others did. The bulbs burned out in just hours.

Another inventor named Joseph Swan had developed the bulb but hadn't been able to solve its short-life problem. Carefully inspecting one of the burned-out bulbs, Mr. Edison told Jimmie and the other lab staff members, "We need to make a long-life bulb that can be powered by an electric generator."

"Why do you want to work on another man's project?" a new worker asked.

Without a bit of hesitation, Mr. Edison said, "I'm always on the lookout for novel ideas that others have used successfully, because even when successful, we don't know one-millionth of 1 percent about anything. Every idea is original if you adapt it to the problem you're working on."

Jimmie had lost count of how many nights the staff had worked trying to find a bulb filament that didn't burn up so fast. The boss had even hired a German glassblower named Ludwig Boehm. He made glass bulbs with the air pumped out of them because the boss knew filaments would burn longer in an airless vacuum.

Right off, Jimmie liked Ludwig, especially after his run-in with Wallace. The glassblower had come to work his first day and was setting up a gas burner and other equipment on a table close to Jimmie's. Carefully handling his tools, the German hardly noticed what looked like a pile of black-and-white wool in a nearby corner. He had just started heating a glass rod when Jimmie saw the black-and-white pile get up and walk over to the new man. Feeling a soft rub on his leg and hearing some sniffing, Ludwig looked down. "Aaaaaah!" he yelled as he dropped the glass.

The yell and splintering glass caused the pile of wool to run back to its corner.

Jimmie couldn't help laughing as he came over to the startled newcomer. "That's just Wallace. He's one of our lab pets."

"He's so huge!" Ludwig said as he calmed down.

"I know. He's a St. Bernard," Jimmie said. "But he wouldn't hurt you. Here, come on over, and I'll introduce you."

Petting the large dog's head, Ludwig laughed at himself. "What a *dummkopf* I am!"

The German's good humor made it easy for Jimmie to like the new man. But it was Ludwig's first all-night shift that got the rest of the staff to appreciate him. When the men worked into the early morning hours, the boss always ordered the night watchman to bring cheese, crackers, butter, and ham to the lab. Inevitably the food started a party. Munching on crackers and chewing on ham, Jimmie listened as the men told tall tales. After finishing off the late-night snack, James and Francis cleared a table and started arm wrestling. When James lost, Batch went over to the pipe organ and played, "My Poor Heart Is Sad with Its Weeping."

Jimmie and the others laughed but soon were singing the song's words along with Batch. Ludwig joined in, too, though half the time he sang in German! Later Jimmie saw him get up and go over to the shelves where the men kept their personal stuff. He brought back a weird-looking box with lots of strings stretched across it. After he sat down, Jimmie leaned over and asked, "What's that?"

"It's a zither," he said.

Listening to the men sing, Ludwig started plucking out the song on the instrument's stings. The soft, soothing tones soon caused the group to stop singing and just listen. When the German finished, everyone clapped, and Francis said, "Ludwig, you brought a bit of heaven right into the lab."

After a bit more socializing, Jimmie, Ludwig, and the others returned to their lab tables, ready to start work again. As more and more midnights echoed with songs and laughter, followed by long hours of experiments, Jimmie heard that a professor called Mr. Edison and his men the "The Insomnia Squad."

Jimmie thought of the name as he watched yet another filament burn out after only a few minutes. He felt incredibly tired. *How much longer can Mr. Edison and the rest of us continue this?* he thought.

Chapter Seven
SIX THOUSAND TRIES!

Menlo Park, 1879

W e need to try something else," Mr. Edison told his new inventor.

Jimmie nodded, feeling different— more important somehow. Though the boss had often talked to him of needed changes, he'd always been an apprentice. Now he was a real inventor, his four years of service behind him. "It's true the platinum base isn't working as you'd hoped," Edison said. "Though the bulbs with platinum filaments burn longer than Swan's first ones, they still aren't practical for wide use."

Wrestling with the problem of a new filament base, Jimmie thought of the things that had increased the bulb's life so far. Ludwig's glass vacuums had helped a lot. Without air, the filaments no longer gave off gases that expanded and cracked it and the glass. But even with this help, none of the combinations burned more than a few hours.

"Let's try carbon—good, old, faithful carbon."

Mr. Edison's suggestion made sense to Jimmie.

When Batch heard it, he nodded in agreement and said, "It's well worth a try. It's worked for us before."

"I'll go out and get some from the shed," Jimmie volunteered.

As Jimmie left the lab and headed for the shed on the property's back boundary line, he thought, *Maybe carbon will do the trick. . . .*

Even before he got to the building, he could smell the oil lamps. Rows of them were burning, gathering soot on their glass chimneys. Workers were scraping off the black crust from some cold lamps while others were pressing the powder into small, round molds. Wherever telephones were being installed, manufacturers bought the carbon disks to put in their transmitters.

Jimmie went over to one of the soot-scrapers and said, "Mr. Edison needs some loose carbon. He wants to try using it on light filaments."

"Now, that's a switch," the worker said as he dumped a couple of bowls of the black powder into a jar. "Out here, the carbon comes after the light, not before it!"

The jar Jimmie brought back to the lab started another round of late-night experiments. By mid-October everyone had done so many carbon experiments that no amount of soap could wash the black from under their fingernails or out of the lines in their hands.

Adding another layer of black to his hands, Jimmie rolled and kneaded a piece of cotton thread in a soot-and-tar mixture. He'd spent hours grinding the powder until it was finer than the finest flour. Nimbly, his fingers rolled and turned and pinched the thread into the black mixture. Finally he gave it to Mr. Edison to put in the furnace.

Jimmie slept the rest of the night and had just splashed water on his face when the boss took the thread out of the carbonizing furnace. Walking over with the towel still in his hand, he saw Mr. Edison pick up what looked like a long, black hair. "Is that the thread?" he asked.

"Yes, it is. Now we'll attach it to the wires molded into Ludwig's bulb stem."

Even though Jimmie had seen it done a thousand times, he still couldn't pull himself away. With utmost care, Mr. Edison attached the black filament to the wires and then placed one of Ludwig's bulbs over the top of the connecting stem.

Jimmie took back the towel and returned just as Francis was putting the newly made bulb on a vacuum pump. Mr. Edison sat on a chair and watched the air-sucking process. While waiting, Jimmie asked, "What are you going to try next?"

"When I was out West last year, someone threw a broken bamboo fishing pole into the fire. Its fibers burned with a bright intensity. Perhaps we'll try that. . . . Maybe we'll even send someone to Japan for fresh bamboo. . . ."

"It's done, Al," Francis interrupted. "I've sealed off the bulb."

"Record the time," Mr. Edison said. "Note that this test began on October 19."

The rest of the staff was gone because they'd been up all night, but Jimmie's nap had left him wide awake. Throughout the morning he worked on another filament made from a mixture with more tar. Four hours later, he noticed the bulb was still burning. "Hey, boss, it looks like this is going to be one of the longer burning bulbs," he yelled.

Mr. Edison nodded but didn't get excited. It was just one more of hundreds of experiments.

When Jimmie looked up from his work four hours later, he wasn't so sure. Walking over to the bulb, he studied it for any sign that the filament was burning up. He saw none. Looking up, he saw Mr. Edison standing beside him. "This is definitely one of the better filaments," he told Jimmie.

When Jimmie awoke the next day the bulb still burned brightly. The staff had returned, and he heard comments: "It's been more than twenty-four hours!" "Can this be it?"

"Maybe all this black under our fingernails won't be for nothing."

Throughout the day Jimmie and the others frequently checked the light's filament to see if it was disintegrating. They no longer said anything but simply grinned and gave the thumbs-up sign.

At two o'clock on the morning of October 21, more than forty-five hours later, Mr. Edison checked the filament's condition. Looking up, he flashed the biggest smile Jimmie had seen since his first phonograph had repeated Sarah Hale's poem. "We've done it, men!" he shouted. "The filament is still intact."

Jimmie and the others cheered and clapped while the boss increased the voltage until the filament burned up.

When Mr. Edison took the burned bulb apart, he said, "If this will burn more than forty hours now, I know we can make one that burns a hundred!"

For the next three weeks, everything that anyone could imagine was carbonized. Jimmie tried all kinds of paper and cardboard. Batch worked with twines while Francis experimented with wood fibers and Charles tackled vegetable fibers. The boss even sent men to Japan, China, and other parts of the world in search of the ideal carbonizing material. Jimmie heard Stockton Griffin, the boss's secretary, say, "According to the records, we've tried more than six thousand different types of filaments!"

Looking at the continuously burning bulbs now being tested, Jimmie thought, *It was worth every last test!*

Chapter Eight
FLIP THE SWITCH

Menlo Park, 1880 to 1882

"Well, I'll be," Mr. Edison said as he leaned back in his chair and scratched his head. "The fishing pole works best!"

Jimmie wiped lamp blacking from his hands and walked over to look at a glowing bulb that was burning longer than all the others had. "Is that the one with the bamboo in it?" he asked.

"Yes, and it's lasted more than one hundred hours," Mr. Edison answered as he leaned forward to take another look at the fragile, charred fiber dangling between the bulb's two upright wires. "This should do it! Every home and business can now have long-lasting light."

Jimmie knew his boss's dream, but it all seemed so far-fetched. Even with the new bulb, electric lighting wouldn't just happen. *It took weeks to wire our laboratory and install an electricity-producing generator,* he thought. *It will take forever to string wire and build generators all over the country!*

As more of the staff gathered around to see the bamboo bulb, Jimmie's worry was lost amid more practical questions. "Do you want to take out a new patent?" "Where can we get a steady supply of bamboo?" staff members asked.

"You could always try Woolworth's Five and Ten Store," Francis said with a laugh. "To hear my wife talk about the new place, you'd think you could buy anything ever wanted for a nickel or dime!"

After the laughter and talk died down, Charles Batchelor suggested everyone get a good night's sleep. "Tomorrow we begin lighting America," he said with a smile.

Five weeks later, Jimmie and the others were working on a better process for making the bulbs and "Jumbo." The last invention fit its name, which came from P. T. Barnum's huge circus elephant. Jumbo was a giant, electricity-producing dynamo powered by a steam engine. Mr. Edison planned to

start lighting America by powering up the block in New York City that held millionaire J. P. Morgan's offices and the *New York Tribune* building.

Days turned into weeks and months as the boss pushed for electrical lighting. He ordered more Jumbo dynamos made, sent Batch to establish electric lighting in Paris, and bought buildings in New York to house the Edison Electric Illuminating Company. He sent Jimmie to work at the new company.

After unpacking in his newly rented room in New York, Jimmie wished he could still visit with Mrs. Edison and play with the children, Dot, Dash, and Little William. But Mrs. Edison wasn't feeling too well these days, and now that Jimmie was an employee, not an apprentice, he could easily afford rent. Besides, he lived close enough to the company to walk to work.

Starting the first electric district was all the work that Jimmie had imagined it would be. It took three months just to get all the bugs out of the thirty-one-ton Jumbo dynamo that was connected to six engines and powered by two huge steam boilers. In addition, the boss didn't want his electrical wires above ground.

A forest of utility poles already crisscrossed parts of the city, and everything from telephone wires to burglar-alarm wires dangled above the hot arc street lighting. More than one repairman had been killed while working on the maze of uninsulated wires.

Steering clear of the dangerous mess, Mr. Edison had Jimmie and others working on an underground system that would radiate out from the power station like octopus arms. To protect the electric cables, they were wrapped in hemp string and placed in cast-iron pipes. "Fill the pipes with this asphalt mixture that the Menlo Park lab concocted," Mr. Edison told Jimmie. "The lines should last fifty years."

After the foul-smelling mixture was poured into every wire-filled pipe, Jimmie allowed the workmen to cover the trenches and bury them under the cobblestone streets and sidewalks.

Once the cables rested safely underground, Mr. Edison and Jimmie started the men wiring the block's buildings. Besides pulling wires up and through walls, fixtures to hold the light bulbs had to be installed too. The boss gave each of his first electric customers a dozen bulbs free, but after that they cost one dollar each.

After almost two years of work, Jimmie couldn't help feeling proud the day he walked beside Mr. Edison to J. P. Morgan's offices at 23 Wall Street. Once inside, he glanced at the new fixtures and found himself wondering, *Will they really start glowing in just a few minutes?*

The clock on the main office wall ticked, and its longer arm jerked past another few minutes. "Just sixty more seconds," the boss told Mr. Morgan and the many reporters gathered around them. "My chief electrician is to throw the main switch at exactly three o'clock."

When the wall clock ticked again, everybody was silent. As usual, Jimmie held his breath. *Oh please, let it work,* he thought.

Suddenly, "in a twinkling," as one reporter put it, the whole area lit up with a soft glow as around the block four hundred lamps flipped on.

For the next couple of hours, folks kept coming in to congratulate Mr. Edison and exclaim over the lighted rooms. Amid smiles and handshakes, Mr. Edison turned aside long enough to tell Jimmie, "Head over to the *New York Tribune's* office and check on the lighting there."

Walking in the fast-darkening dusk, Jimmie noticed that the home-going work crowd kept stopping to look at the yellow glows coming from the block's many windows. When he got to the Tribune office, he found the reporters still marveling at their new world. "There's no harsh glare," one said.

"I know," another replied. "Even now that it's getting dark, I can clearly see what I'm working on."

In order to make the complete report Mr. Edison expected, Jimmie went around and checked each porcelain socket and bulb. Without much surprise, he noted that all worked well. He knew the ecstatic reporters would have told him of any failures.

Jimmie took his time walking back to the Edison offices. All the work, all the effort, had been worth it. No longer did the idea of lighting the country seem so far-fetched. He knew it would be real someday.

Who could have guessed, he thought, *that Thomas Alva Edison, the man who saved my life and burned up a baggage car, would one day light America and change it with his inventions!*

Epilogue
LIGHTS, CAMERA, ACTION!

West Orange, New Jersey

Dear Father and Mother,

I must write and tell you of Mr. Edison's latest invention. He calls it a "kinetoscope," but it is best described as a moving picture! I know it seems impossible, but the boss has had us, "The Insomnia Squad," working on the project day and night. We string photographs together and move them so quickly that the people in the pictures look like they are moving.

The boss has been working with George Eastman to develop a better moving-picture camera and film. We even built a movie studio called the "Black Maria." The boss records vaudeville and circus artists. We got to see Annie Oakley and Bill Cody perform in the studio!

Just today, Mr. Edison handed me a drawing, saying, "I think we can attach a phonograph to the moving pictures. If it works, we can make talking, as well as moving, pictures."

This new idea should not surprise me, but I still am amazed at Mr. Edison's inventions. Since I came back to the laboratory after finishing work on the electric lighting in New York, we have kept busy making wax records, alkaline storage batteries, a copy machine, a dictating machine, a cement mixer, a microphone, and even an electric car! They might be 99 percent perspiration and only 1 percent inspiration, but Mr. Edison is a genius!

The more I get to know the boss's new wife, the more I like her. Mina is not as young and frail as Mary was before she died of typhoid. It is hard to imagine the boss with six children since he didn't spend a lot of time with his first three. But with Mina's three and his three, that is his challenge.

With all the late hours I keep, I have become quite fond of the new drink Coca-Cola. I did a bit of research on it and found out that John Pemberton started selling it right before we moved our laboratory to West Orange, New Jersey, in 1886. He claimed it would cure upset stomachs, headaches, and lift the spirits. I can prove none of this, but it does seem to keep me going on less sleep.

Speaking of which, I should undoubtedly get to bed, as I will be working on improving the movie camera tomorrow. But before I close this letter, I would like to thank you for sending me to be Mr. Edison's apprentice so many years ago. I know it wasn't easy for you to let me go, but it gave me a job I truly enjoy. I have been a part of many changes in our country. I have also had the great opportunity to work beside an incredible man—the Wizard of Menlo Park, Thomas Edison.

Sincerely,

Your son, James

Hope

Character Building with Thomas Edison

Hope:

Expecting Good Things to Happen

When things go wrong, do you give up? If you strike out at baseball, misspell too many words on your school paper, or forget to take out the garbage two days in a row, do you get discouraged? Or do you want to try even harder? If you're a hopeful person, you look ahead, not behind. You focus on what you can do better, not what you've failed to do.

Being hopeful is more than being in a good mood. It's taking action toward making something better. And it can have powerful effects.

Look at Thomas Edison. He was incredibly hopeful. When an experiment failed 100, 1,000, *6,000* times, did he give up? Did he get depressed? Did he throw in his inventor's apron and take up a new line of work? No way! He learned from his mistakes and worked on. He believed good things would happen eventually. And he was right!

Thomas Edison was credited with more than 1,000 original inventions—more than any other inventor in history. He created gadgets that brightened, helped, and entertained the world. And he also inspired the people around him. He could never have accomplished all he did without his fifty hard-working coworkers!

From Telegraph to Light Bulb with Thomas Edison told us about the inventor's journey to fame and achievement. Let's take a look at the character quality that helped him get there.

News Butcher

Without hope men are only half alive.
With hope they dream and think and work.
CHARLES SAWYER

1. After a railway accident, Thomas Edison lost some of his hearing. He might have seen this as a hindrance, but he treated it as a benefit. Why?

_____

_____

Think about what it would be like to work around fifty other people—talking, dropping stuff, scraping chairs. . . .

2. What scary thing happened when Thomas Edison set up his own laboratory in the train baggage car?

_____

STUCK? *Look back on page 13.*

3. How did Thomas Edison respond to the calamity? Did he give up and go home?

_____

_____

HINT: *Edison's response put him in the right place to save a three-year-old child's life!*

WHAT THE BIBLE SAYS

Read Psalm 147:11
The LORD values those who fear Him,
those who put their hope in His faithful love.

King David tells us that we can be valuable to the Lord. How?

_____

_____

IT'S YOUR TURN

What situation are you discouraged about today? Can you figure out a way to see it as a plus in your life? If you are a slow reader, for example, could you say you remember well what you read?

If you can't figure out something, talk to God about it and ask Him to help you see a positive side to your situation.

CHAPTER TWO

99 Percent Perspiration

Hope and patience are two sovereign remedies for all,
the surest reposals, the softest cushions to lean on in adversity.

ROBERT BURTON

1. What attitude did Thomas Edison have about failed experiments? How did he view what we would call failures?

_____

_____

STUCK? *Look back on page 14.*

2. How did Edison's hopefulness affect his fellow workers?

_____

_____

HINT: *Did Edison's fellow workers get discouraged and quit?*

3. When his workers did feel discouraged, what did Edison sometimes use to lift their spirits?

_____

When you can laugh at your mistakes, you'll have more energy to keep trying.
STUCK? *Actions speak louder than words.*

W H A T   T H E   B I B L E   S A Y S

Read Romans 12:12
Rejoice in hope;
be patient in affliction;
be persistent in prayer.

Does God want His children to be easily discouraged? What qualities does He want us to have when things are hard?

_____

_____

I T ' S   Y O U R   T U R N

Patience is rarely easy. Make a list of things you need to be patient about.

_____

_____

_____

_____

"It Speaks!"

They say a person needs just three things to be truly happy in this world.
Someone to love, something to do, and something to hope for.

TOM BODETT

1. The pet raccoon in Mr. Edison's laboratory never gave up trying to do something. What was he trying to do?

_____

STUCK? *Look back on page 19 of the story.*

2. Thomas Edison invented many useful objects, but Alexander Graham Bell beat him to one. What was it?

_____

HINT: *You see people use it every day!*

3. Edison didn't sulk because someone else made a great discovery. Instead, he had plans to make it even better. How?

_____

_____

Remember the lamp soot.

W H A T   T H E   B I B L E   S A Y S

Read Jeremiah 29:11
"For I know the plans I have for you"
—this is the LORD's declaration—
"plans for your welfare, not for disaster,
to give you a future and a hope."

Israel was defeated as a nation many times. Yet God assured them. What kind of plans did He say He had for them?

_____

_____

_____

I T ' S   Y O U R   T U R N

Did you know God has good plans for you too? Take a minute to thank Him for the things He is sending your way.

_____

_____

_____

_____

A Startling Lamb

Hope arouses, as nothing else can arouse, a passion for the possible.
WILLIAM SLOAN COFFIN, JR.

1. Edison and his men worked long and hard to find the best sound transmitter for the telephone. How many days and nights did they wait for their hope to be rewarded?

_____

STUCK? *Look back on page 24.*

2. After so many days and nights of working on one problem, Mr. Edison got two rewards. He found a good transmitter and he thought of another invention that would also use sound vibrations. What was it?

_____

_____

3. Sometimes hope is rewarded immediately! Which of Edison's inventions worked on the first try?

_____

HINT: *We sing along with these today!*

W H A T   T H E   B I B L E   S A Y S

Read Hebrews 10:23–24
Let us hold on to the confession of our hope without wavering,
for He who promised is faithful.
And let us be concerned
about one another in order to promote
love and good works.

Why does God tell us we can hold on to hope totally and completely?

_____

_____

I T ' S   Y O U R   T U R N

Write down the names of your best friends. What can you do to encourage each of them in something they do?

_____

_____

_____

_____

CHAPTER FIVE

The Wizard of Menlo Park

Hope is not a dream, but a way of making dreams become a reality.
L. J. CARDINA SUENENS

1. People who dream about doing the impossible are in good company. Spending time with them is one way to learn how to dream big dreams yourself. As you review this chapter, write down at least three things Thomas Edison dreamed of creating.

_____

_____

_____

NOTE: *The "Food Creator" isn't one of them!*

2. Dreams don't always require exotic ingredients. Look on page 29 of the story for what Thomas Edison considered essential to good inventing; write down the two things he named.

_____

_____

Do you have the ingredients for good inventing?

W H A T   T H E   B I B L E   S A Y S

Read Mark 10:27
Jesus said, "With men it is impossible,
but not with God,
because all things are possible with God."

Jesus taught that God's power can accomplish many more things than man's can. Write down two things that are impossible for people to do, but easy for God.

_____

_____

I T ' S   Y O U R   T U R N

Did you ever have a relative or friend get very sick, then miraculously recover? What other time have you seen God's power making things possible? Thank Him today for using His power for good things.

_____

_____

_____

_____

The Insomnia Squad

Hope is one of the principal springs that keepS mankind in motion.
THOMAS FULLER

1. While working on electric lighting at all hours of the day and night, Edison kept his workmen from snoring (and entertained) by inventing something that made a horrible noise. What was it, and how did it work?

_____

_____

_____

STUCK? *See page 30 for the answer.*

2. Laughter helped Thomas Edison's workers cope with the pressures of doing something over and over in the hope that it would one day work. Write down two things the crew laughed about.

_____

_____

_____

Laughing is healthy for everyone, whether you're an inventor or not!

W H A T ' S   T H E   B I B L E   S A Y S

Read Isaiah 40:31
But those who trust in the LORD
will renew their strength;
they will soar on wings like eagles;
they will run and not grow weary;
they will walk and not faint.

Thomas Edison used humor to renew the strength of his coworkers. What does this verse tell us will happen to those who trust God for fresh strength?

_____

_____

I T ' S   Y O U R   T U R N

Write down two things that are hard for you to keep trying to work on—math, kicking goals, practicing an instrument. . . . Now try and think of a way to turn each thing into a game or something fun. Ask your parents or friends if you're stuck.

_____

_____

Six Thousand Tries!

Hope is the positive mode of awaiting the future.
EMIL BRUNNER

1. Being hopeful involves good judgment. Thomas Edison knew what projects were worth pouring energy into. What discovery in this chapter required lots and lots of effort?

_____

HINT: *You screw it into a socket.*

2. Write down three materials Edison's workers tried before they found the right one.

_____

_____

_____

HINT: *Look back on page 37.*

3. Write down three things that you couldn't do if we didn't have light bulbs.

_____

_____

Thomas Edison sure made life easier!

WHAT THE BIBLE SAYS

Read Hebrews 11:1
Now faith is the reality of what is hoped for,
the proof of what is not seen.

What are three things you are certain of, even though you don't see them?

_____

_____

_____

_____

IT'S YOUR TURN

It isn't always easy to have faith. How do you keep hoping when all seems hopeless? Do you talk to God? Do you talk with friends? Do you read your Bible? Ask God to help keep your faith strong.

CHAPTER EIGHT

Flip the Switch

Hope is an adventure, a going forward, a confident search for a rewarding life.
FRED O. HENKER

1. Thomas Edison's desire to "light America" began on a New York City street block. What two buildings were lit first?

_____

If you were Edison, what would you have lit up first with your new invention?

2. To get electricity into a city's homes meant building huge machines to generate the electricity. What name did they give Edison's first huge machine?

_____

We now use the word to mean "very big."

3. Where did Thomas Edison get the name for his gigantic electricity-producing machine?

_____

HINT: You'll have to go to the circus to get this answer!

4. Of all Thomas Edison's inventions mentioned in this story, which is your favorite?

_____

WHAT THE BIBLE SAYS

Read Colossians 3:23–24
Whatever you do, do it enthusiastically,
as something done for the Lord and not for men,
knowing that you will receive the reward of an inheritance
from the Lord—you serve the Lord Christ.

What do these verses tell us about hard work and who rewards us for it?

_____

_____

_____

IT'S YOUR TURN

Write down two things that make you feel good about doing them. Thank God for this feeling of reward that He gives us.

_____

_____

_____

_____

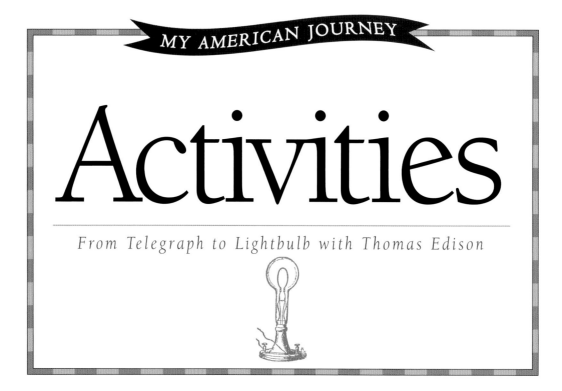

Activities

From Telegraph to Lightbulb with Thomas Edison

Apprentices

To Work with Famous Inventors.

The king of inventors, Thomas Edison, needs help in his lab. You are just the kind of person he loves to work with—energetic, quick-thinking, curious, and eager to create amazing, life-changing gadgets.

Welcome to the world of invention.

As you do the activities in this book, you'll learn how a real inventor works. You'll use the tools Edison used and re-create some of his earliest inventions. Along the way be sure and answer the puzzle question in each activity. Then transfer your answers to the correct places on the last page, so you can solve the crossword puzzle. If you've got what it takes to finish this book, you'll become a *My American Journey* Apprentice Inventor.

The Invention

Ambitious people like Tom Edison needed lots of tools and help to produce their inventions. He stored his tools and employed his fellow inventors in his laboratory. Thomas Edison had three "invention factories" or laboratories during his lifetime. As you walk in the door of his Menlo Park lab, does the chemical smell tickle your nose? Are you surprised at the number of books and jars of materials you see? Can you feel the "electricity" of minds at work?

Laboratory

The lab is where inventions change from ideas to reality. Edison's second-floor lab housed fifty men at fifty work stations. These benches and tables were crowded with liquid batteries, telegraph and telephone equipment, microscopes, magnifying glasses, melting pots, long-necked beakers—and lots of pencils with teethmarks on them!

Micrometer

An inventor used this instrument for measuring. They would insert an object into the micrometer's "jaws" and tighten the handle. Measurements on the side told how thick the object was.

Machine Shop

A steam engine on the first floor produced the electricity to run Edison's electric tools, such as lathes and saws. Men powered the others: drills, hammers, files, forges. Using these tools, the machinists created cranks, boxes, rods, gears, and other parts of each new invention.

Glass Blowers

Men shaped melted glass by blowing air into it through a four-foot-long hollow pipe. They then shaped the resulting bubble with paddles and other molding tools. One shape that came out of Thomas Edison's laboratory became the light bulb!

Chemists

Chemists occupied the second floor of Edison's lab. The walls were lined, from floor to ceiling, with more than 2,500 bottles of chemicals. Edison had almost that many ideas!

All of Edison's workers dressed up. They wore derby hats, stiff collars buttoned on white shirts, bow ties, and many had well-trimmed mustaches. This made the inventors look like ordinary people.

In the 1700s and 1800s many young people worked and lived with a master craftsman in order to learn a skill. Look in the "Did You Know?" section for what this young person was called. (#1)

— — — — — — — —

Dots and Dashes

In Edison's time, you couldn't call a friend who lived in another town on the phone. You either had to write a letter, visit, or send a telegram. The invention of the telegraph made immediate communication over long distances possible. Edison called it "writing with lightning." By his fifteenth birthday, telegraph lines stretched all across the country. No wonder the future inventor quickly built his own and learned how to work this latest wonder.

Look in the "Did You Know?" section of this book and find what word was used to refer to any type of code communication that used clicks or lights. (#2)

_ _ _ _ _ _ _ _ _ _

Telegraph

This invention finally made communication faster than post-office deliveries. An operator translated a message into a code of long and short clicking noises that represented letters and numbers. By tapping a lever attached to wires, he clicked out each message. Electricity carried the message to another operator, who listened to the clicks and translated them into a readable message. This message is called a telegram.

The Morse Code

This special alphabet and punctuation code was made up by an American named Samuel Morse. Using Morse's dots and dashes, words can be spelled out over telegraph lines or even by flashing lights. A dot is a quick click of the telegraph key; a dash is twice as long as a dot. Many years after Samuel Morse's death, the original code was slightly changed. Today the revised dots and dashes are called The International Morse Code.

THE MORSE CODE

A	B	C	D	E	F
. ▬	▬ . . .	. . . .	▬ . .	.	. . ▬ .

G	H	I	J	K	L
▬ ▬ .	. . . .	. .	. ▬ ▬ ▬	▬ . ▬	. ▬ . .

M	N	O	P	Q	R
▬ ▬	▬ .	▬ ▬ ▬	. ▬ ▬ .	▬ ▬ . ▬	. ▬ .

S	T	U	V	W	X
. . .	▬	. . ▬	. . . ▬	. ▬ ▬	▬ . . ▬

Y	Z	1	2	3	4
▬ . ▬ ▬	▬ ▬ . .	. ▬ ▬ ▬ ▬	. . ▬ ▬ ▬	. . . ▬ ▬	. . . . ▬

Telegraphers

Traveling telegraph operators (or "tramp telegraphers") like Tom had a rough life. Often working in dank, windowless offices, Tom battled roaches, rats, and disease. To relieve the misery, Tom became an expert prankster, startling his fellow workers into much-needed laughter.

Create a Message Using Morse Code

Try using Morse Code to communicate. First write down a short message you'd like to send a friend. Now, using the Morse Code symbols above, translate each letter into the correct combination of dots and dashes. This is what your message would look like at a telegraph office before someone translated it into regular letters.

Pranks and Gadgets

Tom Edison knew how to have fun. As an inventor he put all his creativity to work—and to play. He made useful gadgets and pulled surprising pranks. He never seemed to run out of ideas. As an apprentice in his laboratory, you would never be bored. And you'd always want to keep an eye on the boss!

Electric Pen

This pen provided a cheap, easy way for businesspeople to make copies of letters and such. It had a fast needle that moved up and down, powered by a small motor. As someone "wrote" with it, it punched many small holes in the paper. When finished "writing," the secretary put a clean sheet of paper beneath the punctured one. He or she then used a roller to spread ink across the punched sheet. Drops of ink went through the small holes and marked the paper below. When the inked and punched paper was lifted off, the sheet below contained the original written letter.

The electric pen was the first of many duplicating devices; from it we progressed to carbon paper, mimeograph machines, copy machines, and scanners.

Corpse Retriever

Edison's coinventors often fell asleep after long days at their workbenches. If one of them started snoring too loud, Edison would apply his corpse retriever: an uncovered soapbox mounted on a ratchet wheel. As one turned the crank there arose a racket like a tornado in a tunnel, and the sleeper slept no more!

Electric Train

Tom was so thrilled with electricity that he wanted to use it with all kinds of machines. He put together an electric locomotive whose rails were electrically wired. The engine drew current from its wheels. Many visited Tom's Menlo Park laboratory (above) just to see it work.

Tom Edison used his "rat paralyzer" on other pesky critters. What were they? Look on page 16 in *From Telegraph to Lightbulb with Thomas Edison* to find out. (#3)

— — — — — — — — — — — —

Water Bucket & Dipper

Before water coolers were invented, businesses used water buckets to supply workers with drinks. Edison's lab had one of these buckets, and beside it a dipper hung on a nail next to a sign that asked its users to "Please return the dipper." After Tom wired the nail to a battery, each drinker got a shock!

Rat Paralyzer

When a tramp telegrapher, Tom wanted to get rid of a bunch of rats that had overrun one of the small, dark rooms he was forced to work in. So he rigged up two metal plates to a battery. He put the plates close together but not touching and then left a bit of food on one of them. When a rat came to eat the food, it usually put its front feet on one plate and its back feet on the other. When it did, it completed the electric circuit and was "fried" or electrocuted.

Needles and Cylinders

Thanks to Tom Edison, we can listen over and over to our favorite music groups, books, and even phone calls we miss. We can even record our own voice and play it back! The voice and sound recordings that Edison started, using clunky round cylinders, are made today with MP players, tapes, and compact discs.

Enrico Caruso

Disk Records

Disks were even hardier and longer-lasting than wax records. From Edison's first disk records, we progressed to long-playing albums, reel-to-reel tapes, eight-track tapes, small and handy cassettes, compact discs, and finally MP payers which have the clearest sound available.

Early Performers and Songs

Scott Joplin, the ragtime composer, and Enrico Caruso, an early opera singer, were among the first to make records to be played on the newfangled phonograph. Titles of some of Edison's early recordings were: "I'm Sitting on Top of the World," "Croon a Little Lullaby," "Sally's Not the Same Old Sally," and "Just Rolling Along."

Old Phonographs

All early phonographs had these components in common: a hand crank, a needle (or stylus), a speaker (first an elongated horn, later modified into a small panel on the machine), and a turntable. Some phonographs were transported in a handsome carrying case; others were kept on display in one room of the house, much like TVs are today.

Wax Records

This smaller (2 inches) cylinder was made of wax and lasted longer than the foil invention. Wax doesn't tear! These records originally stored 100 grooves of sound per inch; they were later improved and their playing time doubled. But soon Edison wanted to improve these too.

W hen testing the new phonograph, why did Edison hold a piece of metal in his teeth? Look back on page 22 to find out what he hoped to feel through the metal. (#4)

_ _ _ _ _ _ _ _ _ _

Edison's Phonograph

The first record was a 4-inch-wide cylinder drum with tinfoil wrapped around it. A needle reacted to sound and made vertical impressions on the foil as the cylinder was hand-cranked at about sixty revolutions per minute. It was the only Edison invention that worked the first time, and it was his favorite.

A Bright Idea

Every inventor needs not just ideas, but the patience to pursue them. Few of Edison's inventions worked easily, and his crew often waded through hundreds of experiments to find the correct components to keep a contraption running. A good inventor sees the long process not as wasted time but as valuable—even fun!

Complete a Circuit

You will need: 1.5 volt battery
1.5 volt bulb with a bulb holder
Coated wire and wire strippers
A thick piece of cardboard
2 brass paper fasteners
A paper clip

1) Cut two pieces of wire. Use the wire strippers to strip off the ends. 2) Take one end of each wire and attach it to each battery terminal.
3) Attach one of the wires from the battery to one end of the bulb holder. 4) Cut a 2"x2" piece of cardboard for the base of your switch. Wrap the other wire from the battery around a paper fastener and push it through the cardboard. 5) Cut a 3rd piece of wire and strip both ends. Attach one end to the other paper fastener and push it through the cardboard an inch from the first fastener. Attach the other end of the wire to the light bulb base.
6) Now, attach the paper clip to one paper fastener so that it will swivel and touch the other fastener. You have closed the circuit, the bulb should light!

Different Light bulbs

The lighting that enables you to read this book began with Edison's carbon-filament light bulb; then came the tantalum-filament light bulb followed by a drawn-wire-filament light bulb with tip. Inventors went on to try gas-filled bulbs with tips and vacuum bulbs without tips. Finally people developed the inside-frosted bulb we use now.

Making use of Black Soot

In Tom's fast-moving mind, oil lamps could do more than light his desk. They could help him light a city! Using carbon—the black soot scraped from the lamps' glass chimneys—the inventor coated and charred hundreds of materials in order to find a light-bulb filament that wouldn't burn out when hot electricity ran through it. Finally he tried carbonizing cotton sewing thread and it worked! But Edison didn't stop there. He went on to try 6,000 materials in order to find an even longer burning light bulb.

Shedding a Little Light on a President

The White House was wired with electric lights when President Benjamin Harrison was in office. But even with lighting at his fingertips, he and his wife never flipped a switch. Both were afraid of electricity, so they let the servants turn the light switches on and off!

First Lady, Mrs. Benjamin Harrison

The Electric Motor

Once houses and businesses were wired for electricity, manufacturers started putting electric motors on everything—washing machines, vacuums—to name a few. Above, a man wires a large motor.

Underground Cable

Tom Edison realized that stringing his electric lighting cables above the ground was too dangerous. Too many uninsulated cables already hung there. Instead he wrapped his cables in hemp, then threaded them through cast-iron pipes, which were filled with a concoction of asphalt, linseed oil, paraffin, and beeswax. Then the cables were buried. They worked, and they lasted much longer than the ones above ground.

Look in the "Did You Know ?" section of this book and find out what is made from an iron rod and coils. (#5) HINT: *Big ones can pick up a car!*

— — — — — — — — — — — —

Moving Pictures

Lights! Action! Camera! Today a movie can earn millions of dollars. With our incredible sound systems, advanced color photography, and huge movie screens, filmmakers can make you feel like you're right in the middle of the action. In addition, accomplished actors, location filming, stunt people, and computerized images can create heart-stopping aliens and animated bugs. But before all this, moving pictures started out as just an idea in Thomas Edison's mind.

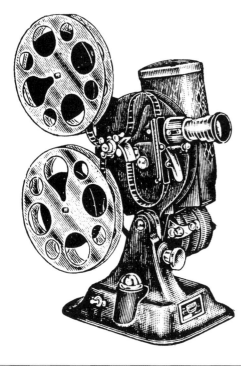

Reel Film

The key to making motion pictures was a sturdy but pliable film called celluloid. Since it could be threaded into long rolls, it enabled the photographer to take many pictures in sequence. Played back at high speed, the images seemed to move.

Early Films

Edison filmed stage acts to begin with—famous performers like Annie Oakley and Buffalo Bill. After a while Edison decided he wanted to create a "living" story by having people act it out. His first popular story film was called The Great Train Robbery. *It ran 10 minutes and featured an exciting story line—the defeat of nasty train robbers by good citizens. Some of the first film celebrities were Charlie Chaplin, Mary Pickford, and Rudolph Valentino.*

Skee the "Did You Know?" section to find out who invented roll film. (#6)

See the "Did You Know?" section to find out who invented roll film. (#6)

George __ __ __ __ __ __ __

Kinetoscope

This invention didn't show movies on big screens like today's projectors do. The kinetoscope was a small, wooden cabinet. To see a motion picture on it, one person at a time peered through a peephole. As he or she watched, a series of photographs was flipped rapidly, making them look like they were moving. These early "films" were short: they lasted only 15 to 60 seconds.

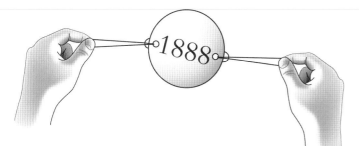

Make a Kinetoscope

You'll need:
A piece of round cardboard 3 inches wide
A hole punch and a marking pen
2 rubber bands

Draw a large 18 on the left-hand side of the cardboard disc. Then flip it over, from bottom to top, and write a large 88 on the right-hand side. Use a hole punch to punch a hole in each side of the disc. Take the end of one rubber band and pull it halfway through one hole. Take the other end of the rubber band and pass it through the middle of the already-threaded one. Pull tight. Do the same on the other side of the disc. Then, by pulling the rubber bands away from the disc, twirl the disc back and forth quickly. You will see the year of Tom Edison's kinetoscope invention—1888—as one number.

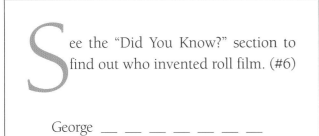

Record of a Sneeze

The first motion picture filmed on a kinetoscope showed a mechanic named Fred Ott in the act of sneezing.

Inventor's Advice

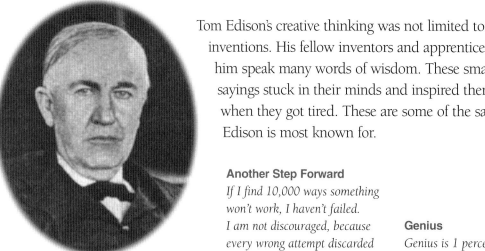

Thomas Edison

Tom Edison's creative thinking was not limited to inventions. His fellow inventors and apprentices heard him speak many words of wisdom. These smart little sayings stuck in their minds and inspired them when they got tired. These are some of the sayings Edison is most known for.

Another Step Forward

If I find 10,000 ways something won't work, I haven't failed. I am not discouraged, because every wrong attempt discarded is another step forward.

Genius

Genius is 1 percent inspiration and 99 percent perspiration. . . . I never did anything by accident, nor did any of my inventions come by accident; they came by work.

Opportunity

There is far more opportunity than there is ability.

Endurance

The first requisite for success is the ability to apply your physical and mental energies to one problem incessantly without growing weary.

L ook back on page 27 to complete Tom Edison's nickname: (#7)

The Wizard of __ __ __ __ __ __ __ __ __

Thinking

It is astonishing what an effort it seems to be for many people to put their brains definitely and systematically to work. . . . There is no expedient to which a man will not go to avoid the real labor of thinking.

Knowledge

Until man duplicates a blade of grass, nature can laugh at his so-called scientific knowledge.

Time

The only time I become discouraged is when I think of all the things I like to do and the little time I have in which to do them. . . . The thing with which I lose patience most is the clock. Its hands move too fast.

Ingredients of an Invention

All you need to be an inventor is a good imagination and a pile of junk.

Perseverance

Many of life's failures are people who did not realize how close they were to success when they gave up. . . . Everything comes to him who hustles while he waits.

Great Inventions

Tom Edison wasn't the only inventor hard at work. Many men were trying to create new gadgets that would change the world. They often built on each other's ideas; whoever patented the final product got credit for it. Edison was issued 1,093 patents, more than any inventor in American history.

Fountain Pen

Lewis E. Waterman created the first fountain pen in 1884. The best part of Waterman's pen was its ink reservoir—a pen you didn't have to dip in an inkwell! Still, you had to fill the reservoir by using an eyedropper, so you still had to carry ink with you.

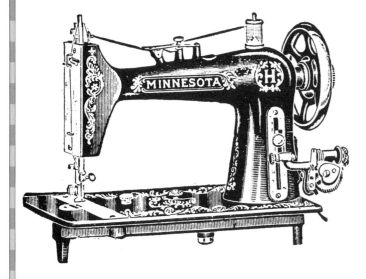

Sewing Machine

Elias Howe helped develop, and received the patent for, the first sewing machine in 1846. What we take for granted—two interlocking threads pushed together by the turn of a crank—was miraculous then. So many people infringed on Howe's copyright that he took his case to court. He profited by more than $2 million before his patent expired in 1867.

Look in the "Did You Know?" section for the first name of the man who invented the telephone. (#8)

— — — — — — — — — —

Graham Bell

Cotton Gin

Slaves removed the seed from cotton fiber until Eli Whitney (left) came along. In 1793 he invented the cotton gin, a hand-cranked machine in which pointed teeth pulled through fiber, separating the seed from the lint. Whitney's invention could put out 50 pounds of clean cotton per day, making cotton a profitable crop for the first time.

Steamship

American inventor, artist, and engineer Robert Fulton created the steamship while in France in 1803. He launched his first American steamboat in 1807 in the New York Harbor. He also did early work on the submarine, but no one was interested in the underwater ship!

Typewriter

In 1868, Christopher Latham Soles developed the first type-writer. The arrangement of letters on the keyboard was called "QWERTY" because that's the first line of letters. The letters were arranged this way to help salesmen sell the machine. Since all the letters of typewriter are in the top line, the salesman could quickly and impressively type out the name of his product for customers.

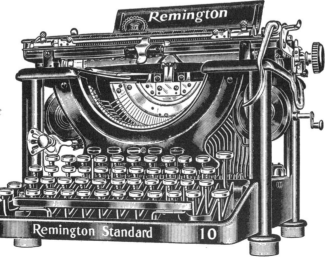

Patents

Putting a patent on an invention identified and protected its inventor. No one else could copy or take credit for it. Provision for patents was written into our Constitution in 1787, but it wasn't until 1790 that an official Patent Board was established. Until 1880 models of inventions had to be submitted with a patent application. Afterward, only drawings were necessary.

Apprentice

This was a young person who worked and lived with a master craftsman to learn a skill. Usually the apprentice was legally bound to his or her master for 4 to 7 years. Our character, Jimmie, would have been one of the last few apprentices in America. After 1850 the apprentice system started to disappear as more and more unskilled workers simply became independent employees.

Arc Lighting

The first electric streetlights used arc lighting. These bright lights were made by jumping large amounts of electric current between two small, pencil-like carbon posts inside a glass bulb. The fiery arc of electricity gave off a brilliant light that was too harsh and strong for rooms or homes.

The Brakeman's job was to stop the train.

Bamboo

This woody member of the grass family can grow from 3 feet to 160 feet high! It has obvious joints from which other leaves or flower clusters grow. Most varieties stand erect and are hollow except at the joints. An incredible fact about this grass is that it can grow up to 24 inches in one day!

Black Maria

Thomas Edison's first moving-picture theater was a 50-foot-long building lined with black tar paper that inspired its name. The building had a hinged roof that could be lifted to allow in natural light. Mounted on a circular track, it could also be rotated to follow the course of the sun. The engineer

who designed it for Edison, W. K. L. Dickerson, said, "This distribution of light and shade are productive of the happiest effects in the films."

Alexander Graham Bell

Though he was an inventor like Thomas Edison, Alexander Graham Bell was also a teacher of deaf children. He opened a school in Boston after immigrating to the United States from Scotland. In his spare time he worked with telegraphs and finally devised the telephone. In his later years he got interested in flight and made

Alexander Graham Bell

Did you

important improvements to the Wright brothers' first successful airplane. He also helped start the National Geographic Society, which today publishes a popular educational magazine.

Brakeman

Also called a "brakie" or "shack," this railroad employee's job was to stop the train. Unlike today's trains, which have automatic braking systems that stop all the cars at once, each train car in the 1800s had to

be stopped separately with its own brake. After the engineer signaled a stop, usually two brakemen went along the train cars' roofs, gradually tightening each brake by turning a wheel on top of the car. In sunshine, rain, sleet, and snow, the brakemen stayed on top of the train, moving from car to car even when the train was coated with ice!

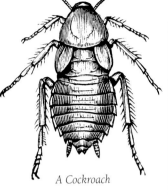
A Cockroach

Centennial Exposition

In 1876 the United States celebrated the one-hundredth birthday of the signing of the Declaration of Independence by holding a world's fair in Philadelphia, Pennsylvania.

Almost 50 other countries helped us celebrate by sending products of art, science, nature, and industry. Close to ten million people came to see incredible inventions such as the telephone, refrigerator car, and duplex telegraph (it could send and receive a message at the same time).

Consumption

In the 1800s this was the common name for tuberculosis, a disease that attacks a person's lungs. In Thomas Edison's day, many people died from it.

Cornet

This brass instrument was popular in the 1800s and early 1900s. In the 1930s, before the trumpet became the most popular, most jazz bands featured cornet players. Though the trumpet and cornet look much alike, the cornet makes a more mellow sound. It also has a funnel-shaped mouthpiece while the trumpet's mouthpiece is cup-shaped.

The Daily Graphic

This New York paper called itself "an illustrated evening newspaper," and it frequently contained articles about Thomas Edison. After he invented the phonograph, one such write-up suggested that a speaking Statue of Liberty might be one of the "awful possibilities for the new speaking phonograph."

Derby

This hardened felt hat has a rounded top with a short, slightly curled-up brim all the way around. An Englishman who made hats, William Bowler, designed the derby in 1850. As a result, his countrymen called the hat a "bowler." But when the Earl of Derby made the style popular by wearing it to horse races, Americans called the hat a "derby."

A Derby

Dummkopf

This German word is used to call oneself or someone else a name. It is similar to our words *dummy* and *blockhead*.

George Eastman

This inventor, who worked with Thomas Edison in creating motion-picture film, made many other contributions to modern-day photography. Until Eastman invented the first roll of film in 1884 and later the inexpensive Kodak camera, taking pictures was a rich man's hobby. But an affordable camera and film soon made photography a popular pastime. In 1892 George Eastman started the Eastman Kodak Company to meet the fast-growing demand for his products.

Edison's Invention Factories

Everything You Ever Wanted to Know about the Time of Thomas Edison

know?

Cockroach

There are more than 4,000 types of cockroaches throughout the world, and most play an important role in the earth's ecology. They eat and break down everything from forest leaves to animal droppings. In turn, many animals eat cockroaches. In spite of their positive role in nature, a few types of cockroaches have invaded homes and given the bug a bad name.

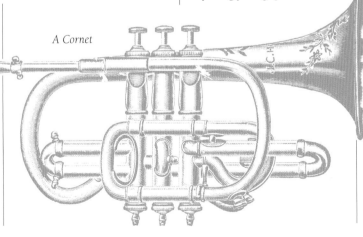
A Cornet

George Eastman

Thomas Edison owned three invention factories from the time he was twenty-three years old until his death. They were located in Newark, New Jersey; Menlo Park, New Jersey; and West Orange, New Jersey. He also owned other property, including the electric power station in New York City and a rubber-growing project in Florida. What money Edison made on his inventions he spent on making new ones.

Electric Pen

This invention created what Thomas Edison called "autographic printing." It provided a cheap, easy way to make copies of letters and other documents. The pen had a fast-moving, up-and-down needle powered by a small motor. As a person "wrote" with it, it punched many small holes in the paper. When the "writing" was finished, a clean sheet of paper was put beneath the punctured one. Then a roller spread ink across the punched sheet. Drops of ink went though the small holes and marked the paper beneath it. When the inked-and-punched paper was lifted off, the sheet below contained the original letter.

Electromagnet

Using the positive and negative charges in electricity, large powerful magnets can be made from iron rods and coils. The bigger the rods and coils and the greater the charge of electricity sent through them, the greater the strength of the magnet. Large electromagnets are used on the cranes that pick up wrecked cars and other scrap metal.

Frank Woolworth

Five-and-Dime Store

In 1879 an American merchant named Frank Woolworth decided to try opening a new kind of store. He'd failed at a number of other businesses but felt sure that a store specializing in items that cost 5 cents and 10 cents would do well. He was right! By 1911 he owned 1,000 such stores throughout the world.

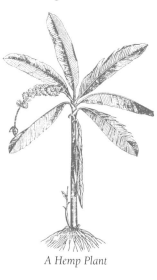

A Hemp Plant

Five Charleses

Many engineers, inventors, metalworkers, chemists, and other professional men worked for Thomas Edison during his sixty years as an inventor. In a picture of his laboratory crew taken in 1880, the caption identifies five men named Charles: Charles L. Clarke, Charles Batchelor, Charles Hughes, Charles Flammer, and Charles Mott.

Foundries

In these workshops or factories, metal is melted and molded into useful objects and machinery parts.

Glassblowing

The art of glassblowing started in the Middle East in the first century. Craftsmen blow molten glass into shapes using a four-foot-long hollow pipe. At one end of the pipe is a mouthpiece. At the other end of the pipe, a small amount of molten glass is gathered. Blowing into the pipe causes the glass to form a bubble. Using paddles and other molding tools, the glassblower forms the bubble into a variety of shapes or objects. Throughout the process the glass is frequently inserted into an open furnace. This constant reheating keeps it flexible until the desired shape is achieved.

An African Elephant

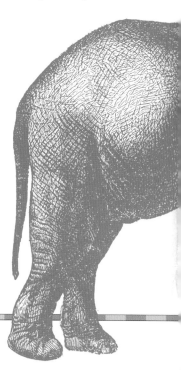

Hemp

The material that Edison wrapped around his first underground electrical wires is actually an herb. The plant, which can grow up to 15 feet tall, has a hollow stem and bark made of strong fibers. Once dried, the fibers are used to make things such as ropes, coarse fabrics, and sailcloth. Originally grown in Asia, it is now cultivated in other parts of the world, including the United States.

Jumbo

This huge elephant was owned by P. T. Barnum, a great showman who started America's first mobile circus. He bought this giant African elephant from the London Zoo and brought it to our country. As the animal's popularity grew, a new word was added to the English language. People started using "jumbo" to describe things that were really big.

"Mary Had a Little Lamb"

This famous poem was written in the 1800s by Sarah Hale, the editor of Godey's Lady's Book. Home-schooled by her mother, Sarah started writing at an early age but never thought of it as a career. Instead, like most women in the early 1800s, she got married and had a family. But then her husband died. She still didn't think her writing could support her four children, so she opened a hat shop. It failed. Only then did she start writing seriously.

Mercury

Also called "liquid silver" or "quicksilver," this natural metallic element is found in the earth mingled with other elements such as silver or cinnabar. At room temperature mercury is a shining, silvery-white liquid. Because it is sensitive to temperatures, it is used in thermometers. Scientist now know that liquid mercury is very poisonous. Though Edison's raccoon played with the silvery element, NO one should today.

Morse Code

Invented by an American named Samuel Morse, this special alphabet and punctuation code is used for simple, long-distance communication. Using Morse's dots and

A Tuning Fork

dashes, words can be spelled out over telegraph lines or even by flashing lights. A dot is a quick click of the telegraph key or lamp shutter while a dash is twice as long as a dot.

Raccoon

This plump, furry animal is found in most of the Americas. It is easy to spot because a stripe of dark fur around its eyes looks like a mask. Its bushy tail is striped with brown-and-black rings. A night animal, the raccoon likes to eat birds, mice, fish, frogs, insects, and eggs. It lives in trees and often doesn't mind being close to towns and cities.

Saint Bernard

This large working dog got its name from rescuing snowbound people who got lost in the Alps. Sent out by the Monks who kept a lodge for travelers near the Great Saint Bernard Pass, which is between Switzerland and Italy, these dogs used their keen sense of smell and direction to locate lost travelers, even those buried in snow.

Telegraphy

Today this term is used rarely and only to refer to the use of a telegraph. However, one hundred years ago people used this word to refer to any form of communication over long distances that was made by using signs or sounds.

Tuning Fork

John Shore, an English trumpeter, invented this small, two-pronged, metal device in 1711. The fork is made of fine metals such as nickel and steel, and it gives off a clear, precise pitch when tapped. Musicians use tuning forks to tune their instruments, but Thomas Edison tried to use the device's sound vibrations in a sewing-machine motor!

A Zither

Zither

Forms of this stringed musical instrument have been around a long time. As early as A.D. 24, Greeks played music by plucking strings stretched flat over a box. The modern zither lies flat on a table (or someone's lap) to be played. It has from 29 to 42 strings, and its player plucks them with both hands.

FILL IN THE BLANKS

Edison's Picture Show

Using the answers from the previous activity pages, work the puzzle below to discover the name of one of Tom Edison's most popular motion pictures.

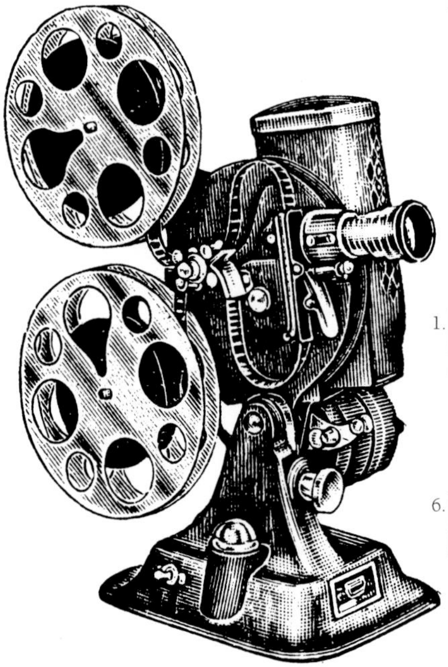

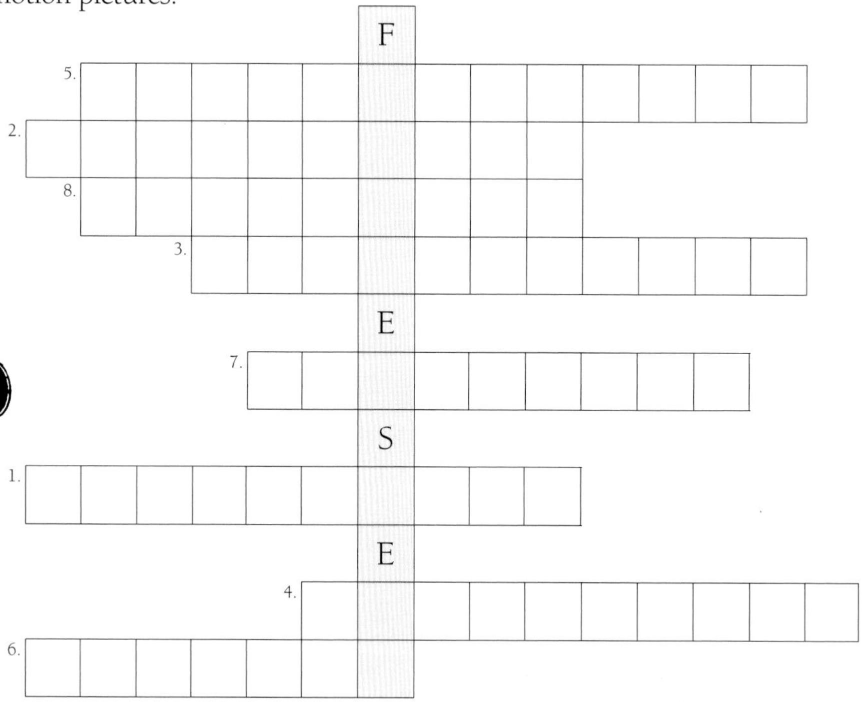

Congratulations!

You've become a MY AMERICAN JOURNEY *Apprentice Inventor!*

Answers to clues: 1. *Apprentice.* 2. *Telegraphy.* 3. *Cockroaches.* 4. *Vibrations.* 5. *Electromagnet.* 6. *Eastman.* 7. *Menlo Park.* 8. *Alexander.* Answer to whole puzzle: *Frankenstein.*